This book belongs to:

· · · · · · · · · · · · · · · · · · ·

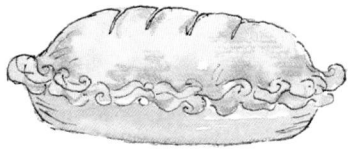

For Ramona and Lisa

First published in Great Britain 2001 by Egmont UK Limited
This edition published 2019 by Dean,
an imprint of Egmont UK Limited,
The Yellow Building, 1 Nicholas Road, London W11 4AN

www.egmont.co.uk

Text and illustrations copyright © 2001 Jan Fearnley

Jan Fearnley has asserted her moral rights

ISBN 978 0 6035 7756 7
70740/001
Printed in Malaysia

Mr Wolf
and the
Three Bears
Jan Fearnley

DEAN

It was a special day for Mr Wolf. He was feeling very excited, because today his friends the Three Bears were coming round for tea.

It was Baby Bear's birthday, and Mr Wolf was planning a lovely party for everyone.

Mr Wolf wanted to cook a special dish for each one of his guests, and because there was such a lot to do, Grandma came along to help.

"We must be tidy and safe in the kitchen when we're cooking," reminded Grandma. "Let's wash our paws before we start, and then we can have some fun."

For Baby Bear's dish, they looked in the big recipe book.
Soon they found the perfect thing to make.

A birthday cake!

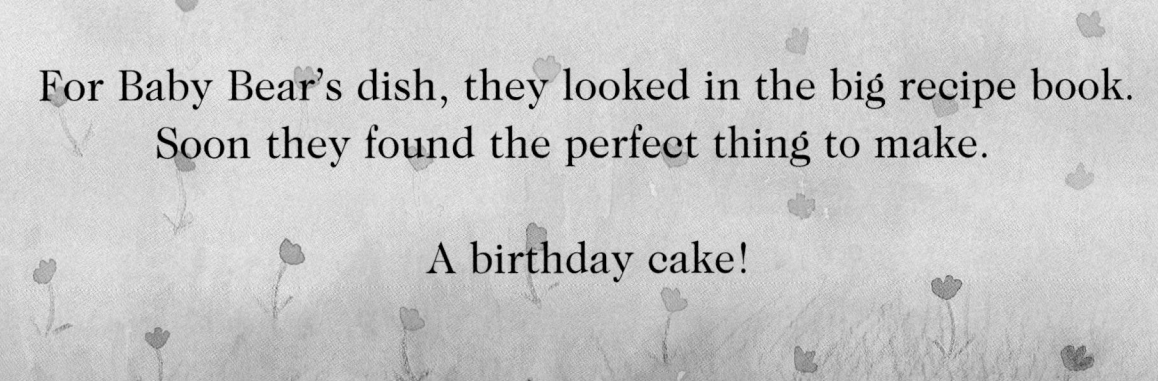

Next they thought about Mummy Bear.
"I know she likes sandwiches," said Mr Wolf.

Grandma remembered there was a recipe in her magazine.

They followed it carefully and soon there was a big heap of sandwiches on the table, all ready for the party.

Now it was time to make something for
Daddy Bear. Grandma's favourite TV programme
gave them lots of ideas.

"Those Huff Puff cakes sound good,"
said Mr Wolf.
"Good thinking," said Grandma.
"We'd better make lots because
he's a big bear."

They were easy to do.

Then it was Grandma's turn to pick something tasty.
But she couldn't decide what she wanted.

Mr Wolf had a brainwave.

Mr Wolf helped Grandma look on the internet
for some ideas and soon found a recipe she
fancied – Cheesy Snipsnaps!

They printed out the recipe and set to work.

Mr Wolf and Grandma still had a lot to do before their guests arrived.

They blew up balloons,

wrapped Baby Bear's present,

laid the table

and made some party hats.

Grandma arranged some flowers.

Then they tidied the house from top . . .

to bottom . . .

until it looked lovely.

"Ready!" said Mr Wolf, just as they
heard a knock on the door.

"Come in! Welcome!" cried Mr Wolf.
"Happy Birthday, Baby Bear!"

But somebody came barging in before them!

IT WAS GOLDILOCKS!

"Let me come in, Mr Wolf," she demanded.
"I smell nice things a-cooking."
"What have you brought her for?"
whispered Mr Wolf. "She always causes trouble."

"She followed us through the woods," said Daddy Bear.
"There was nothing we could do! She said she was
invited too."
"What a fibber!" said Mr Wolf.
"Don't be mean! Let the child come in," called Grandma
from her chair. "But you'd better behave yourself,
Goldilocks," she warned.
"Yeah, yeah," shrugged Goldilocks, tossing her curls.
"I promise."

But it wasn't long before Goldilocks forgot her promise.

When they were dancing, she trod on Mr Wolf's toe
and didn't say sorry.

When they played pass the parcel, Goldilocks took off
all the wrappers instead of just one.

When they played musical chairs,
Goldilocks was too rough – and she cheated!

Grandma didn't join in the games. She just sat in her chair,
as grandmas often do, watching.
"I think it's time for tea," she said. But . . .

. . . someone had got there first!

"Somebody's had a bite out of this cake," said Daddy Bear.

"Somebody's been at this sandwich, too," said Mummy Bear.

"Mine's nearly all gone!" cried Baby Bear.

"This always happens to me!"

"Your food's yukky," complained Goldilocks, with her
cheeks bulging. Her table manners were atrocious!
Poor Mr Wolf. "My party is a disaster!" he whimpered.
Grandma smiled at Mr Wolf and slowly got to her feet.
"It's time for another game," she said.

"Let's play hide and seek."
"Boring," said Goldilocks.
"I always win."
"We'll see," said Grandma.

Everyone ran off to hide.
Grandma counted to one
hundred. "Coming! Ready
or not!" she called.

She took a while . . .

. . . but she did find
everybody eventually . . .

. . . that is, all except
for Goldilocks.
She was nowhere to be seen.

"What a rude girl," said Mummy Bear. "She nearly
ruined our party and now she's gone off without
saying thank you."
"Never mind," said Grandma. "I've got a surprise."
She disappeared into the kitchen . . .

. . . and emerged with a beautiful great big pie,
all steaming hot from the oven, with a golden,
melt-in-the-mouth crumbly pastry crust.

"Clever Grandma!" everybody cheered.

"Let's gobble it up while it's hot!" said Mr Wolf.
"Not just yet," said Grandma.
"I think this is a dish best served cold."

And as they waited for the golden pie to cool,
Grandma giggled to herself and settled back
to enjoy the rest of the party.

"Save me a big piece," she said,
". . . a very big piece.
I'm starving!"